A MOUNTAIN TO CLIMB

REBEL VIPERS MC PREQUEL

JESSA AARONS

A MOUNTAIN TO CLIMB

This book is a work of fiction. The names, characters, places, and incidents are all products of the author's imagination and are not to be construed as real. Any similarities are entirely coincidental.

A Mountain to Climb Copyright ©2023 by Jessa Aarons. All rights are reserved. No part of this book may be used or reproduced in any manner without written permission from the author, except in the case of brief quotations used in articles or reviews. For information, contact Jessa Aarons.

Cover Designer: Charli Childs, Cosmic Letterz Design

Editor: Rebecca Vazquez, Dark Syde Books

TABLE OF CONTENTS

WARNING	V
DEDICATION	VII
PLAYLIST	IX
CHAPTER ONE	1
CHAPTER TWO	7
CHAPTER THREE	13
CHAPTER FOUR	19
CHAPTER FIVE	25
CHAPTER SIX	33
CHAPTER SEVEN	39
CHAPTER EIGHT	45
CHAPTER NINE	51
CHAPTER TEN	61
CHAPTER ELEVEN	65

ACKNOWLEDGMENTS	70
ABOUT THE AUTHOR	72
OTHER WORKS	75

WARNING

This content is intended for mature audiences only. It may contain material that could be viewed as offensive to some readers, including graphic language, dangerous and sexual situations, murder, abuse, and extreme violence.

This story is for all the believers in fate. No matter what life throws your way, know that it's your journey. When you find those great moments, hold on tight to them for as long as you can.

Stay strong and shine on, you crazy diamonds!

PLAYLIST

CLICK HERE TO LISTEN ON SPOTIFY

Made For You – Jake Owen
I'm to Blame – Kip Moore
Head Over Boots – Jon Pardi
When Will I Be Loved – Karla Bonoff, Vince Gill
One of Them Girls – Lee Brice
If I Didn't Have You – Randy Travis
Are You Gonna Be My Girl – Jet
Big, Big Plans – Chris Lane
Puzzle of Us – Adam Doleac
Stay – Ryan Kinder
Last Name – BEXAR

CHAPTER ONE

JETHRO

It's a toss-up. I'm not really sure how I'm feeling just yet. I've been back on American soil for a total of seven minutes, and I don't know if I'm happy or not.

What happened back there, in the Persian Gulf, is definitely going to be with me for the rest of my life. I was fortunate enough to walk off that ship, but several of my fellow sailors weren't so lucky.

My bunkmate, Mike Connors, for one. He just happened to be in the wrong place at the wrong time. It could've been me, but for some unknown reason, it wasn't. His family will be one of many who welcome their service member home inside a pine box. And you want to know what they get for that? A folded-up flag and twenty-one-gun salute. There won't be parades, or parties, or hugs from their babies. His wife and newborn daughter are now alone.

And where am I, you ask? I'm standing here, in Washington, D.C., watching Mike's body being loaded onto another plane. I have no plans for the rest of the night other than a hot shower and a few cold beers.

"Hill." I turn and see our unit chaplain walking toward me. He makes his way across the tarmac and I'm completely clueless as to what he needs from me. I spent many days and nights talking to him about our lives back home, but as soon as we got off the plane, I figured he'd be doing his chaplain duties and not looking for me.

Chaplain Malcom King is one tough son of a bitch. He looks nothing like you'd imagine a man of the cloth would. He's the definition of a walking, talking grizzly bear with buzzed black hair, tan skin, and a permanent scowl on his face. And he doesn't even wear a cross or carry a bible.

"What's up, Father?" I try to say with a serious face, holding out my hand to shake.

"Knock it off with that Father shit, Hill." Malcolm grabs my hand and drags me in for a giant bear hug. He pulls back and the scowl he had on his face for thirty seconds is gone. His blank, straight, no nonsense expression is back in full force.

"Something wrong?"

"I'm gonna need you to come with me to the Commander's office before you leave." He throws a thumb over his shoulder and I look to see a Jeep waiting for us.

"Any idea what for?" I don't think I did anything wrong. I hope not, at least. I only have about a month left before my time in the Navy is done. I've served eight years and am ready to get back home.

"Yea, but I'm under orders not to tell you 'til we get inside. Commander's orders."

I pick up my duffel bag and follow Malcolm to the Jeep. I try to get a read on what this could be about, but his face shows me nothing. I toss the duffel into the back, hop in the passenger seat, and before I can buckle my seat belt, we're flying through the parking lot.

"Whoa! Slow down, speed racer. We just got home. Don't need to be rolling this thing over!" I laugh as we barrel around a corner.

"Dude, I'm gonna be honest with you. I can't fucking wait to get back on my Harley. It's been way too damn long since I've ridden her."

"I've been thinking about getting one myself."

That gets an eyebrow response from Malcolm. "No shit?"

"Yup. With my time being about up, I could use a little reward."

I hear him mumble something but can't make it out over the wind blowing around us. I'm about to ask what he said when we come to an abrupt stop. He throws the Jeep in park and jumps out.

I follow him onto the sidewalk, but before we get very far, Malcolm spins around and I almost collide with him. I catch my footing and take a step back. "Let's head inside. Then you can start making decisions about what you're going to do next."

"Yes, sir." I throw a half-ass salute at him and pull the office building's door open, not caring if it shuts before he follows. What a jackass. Someone needs to fill me in on what the fuck is happening.

"Hill!" I'm really getting sick of my name being yelled out today.

"Commander." I drop my duffel and snap to attention, giving him a proper salute. He's not one to mess around with. He holds the pen that's going to be signing my discharge papers.

"At ease, Hill. Follow me." I pick up my bag again, for the twentieth time, and follow him down the hall. I notice Malcolm following a few steps behind but continue to ignore his presence. The door shuts behind me and I'm now trapped in an office with two stoic men. Neither is saying a word and my fuse has about hit its end.

Not caring that I'm in direct violation of about a dozen military rules, I drop down into the chair in front of the Commander's large desk. "Anyone gonna tell me why I'm here? Or should I start guessing?"

The Commander drops into his own chair and folds his hands on the desktop. "Son. There's no easy way to say this, so I'll just spit it out."

I look back at Malcolm and he just dips his head at me. "What is it?'

"You're going home tomorrow."

I'm confused. "What? I thought I had a month left?"

"I got a call from the Red Cross about three hours before your plane landed. Your mother called in to let you know that your father died last night in a farming accident."

I can hear what he's saying, but I feel the room start to close in around me. What's my mom going to do with the farm now that he's gone? I've never really had any interest in growing corn and soybeans. That's part of why I joined the Navy right out of high school. I left for training the day after I graduated and have only been back a handful of times. Now, I have no idea what to do next.

"Jethro." A hand drops on my shoulder and I look to my right. Malcolm is crouched down next to me. "What do you need?"

"I guess I need to go home." I'm still in shock. What do I need? I need my dad to be alive.

Shit, I didn't even think of my younger brother. Andrew is about two years younger than me and has always been my dad's shadow. I can't imagine what he's going through right now.

"Your discharge paperwork is being signed as we speak and you're booked on a flight to Milwaukee tomorrow morning at oh-eight-hundred. Chaplain King will drive you home shortly and you'll have tonight to pack. He'll also pick you up in the morning and get you to your plane. He has all the necessary details." The Commander keeps talking, and I think I catch the important information, but it's time for me to go.

I stand and salute my Commander one last time. "Thank you, Sir."

"Fair winds and following seas." He salutes back.

It's time for me to get home. Wisconsin, here I come.

CHAPTER TWO

MOUNTAIN

FIVE YEARS LATER

"What the hell are you doing, Roxy?" I walk into my bedroom and see my girlfriend latching a suitcase shut. "And where'd you get that?"

"I can't be here anymore." She looks up at me as she drags said suitcase off the bed, letting it fall with a *thump* to the hardwood floor.

"What're you talking about?" I roar.

"I'm leaving, Mountain," she balls her fists on her hips, and starts tapping her high-heeled boot, "and there's nothing you can do about it." The venom-filled statement comes flying out of her mouth.

I look around the room and notice a few of the dresser drawers are open a bit, and the closet's now half empty. Staring at our bed, I see that she stripped off the sheets and tossed my pillow on the floor. She's normally so anal retentive about keeping things super neat and tidy, it's usually really annoying. Seeing the way she's left things in such disarray is throwing me off even more.

"What do you mean you're leaving? You can't go."

"I can and I am. This is my last bag."

"But we have a son." Holy shit. She's going to take Connor away. Not as long as I'm on this side of the dirt, she ain't. "You can't take him. I won't let you. I'm his father!" Each word I say is coming out louder and louder. I stalk forward and back her ass up against the wall. I stand at six-foot-five and tower over her by a good ways. She won't meet my eyes and I'm not liking this one bit.

She mumbles something quickly, but I can't understand her.

"What'd you say?" I grip her by the chin and make her look up.

"I'm not taking him!" she snaps back.

I drop her chin so fast, almost like she actually bit me. "WHAT!"

Roxy skirts around me and tries to get to the door. I reach it first and slam it shut. The bang makes her freeze and she drops her gaze back to the floor. There's something she's not telling me.

I think I know what it is. "You were just gonna leave without saying anything." I'm dumbfounded. Had I not come home from work early, she would've left without a single word.

"I never wanted to be a mother. You knew that from the beginning. I told you the night we met, I didn't want to ever be tied down. I only agreed to have him because you were so excited. But I can't handle it anymore. The club. The baby. You. It's just too much." She's rambling, scratching her forearms, and pacing back and forth at the end of the bed.

I've had it. If this bitch wants out, she can go. "Leave now. Take whatever you have packed and get the hell out of my clubhouse." I open the bedroom door, grab the suitcase she dropped earlier, and toss it out into the hall. It bounces off the opposite wall and pops open. Roxy runs out of the room and kneels down to jam everything back in. There's so much more I probably should say, but I can't seem to form the words to express my fury.

She finally stands, and with one last look, walks down the stairs.

Walking back into our room . . . scratch that . . . this is just my room now.

Walking back into my room, I shut the door and sit down on the bare mattress.

What am I going to do now? I'm thirty-one years old and have to now raise my son alone. What do I tell Connor?

Speaking of Connor, he should be getting up from his nap soon. I open the door that connects to his bedroom and just look at him for a minute. What kind of mother would just walk out on an innocent child? He's only two years old.

Kicking off my boots so I don't make too much noise, I walk into his room, kneel next to his bed, and place my hand on his tiny back. He squirms a little, so I freeze, but he just rolls over and is still out cold. Now, I can see his handsome face. The older he gets, the more everyone says he's a miniature version of me. We have the same sandy blonde hair and crabby attitudes. The only difference is that he got blue eyes from his mother. I hope that's the only thing he inherits from that bitch.

Knock knock.

I turn my head and see my little brother, Brick, standing in the doorway. I drop a kiss on Connor's forehead and stand up, pointing Brick back into my room and shutting the door behind me.

"Did I see Roxy loading her things and leaving? Tell me I was seeing things."

"Nope. You saw right." I sit back on the bed and run my hands over my hair. It's starting to get long and I need a haircut—another thing I'll have to figure out on my own again.

"Where the hell is she going? Is she coming back?"

"What the hell's with all the questions, Brick? I don't fucking know where the bitch is going. She was packing her shit when I came up to check on Connor. And no, she's not coming back."

"What are . . ." he starts, and I stand to take a swing at him for asking another question.

He holds up his hands in surrender.

"I don't know what I'm gonna do, so you can skip that question. I don't know much, but I do know I'm all that boy has now and he will not be unloved. I'll raise him the best I know how and we're better off without her."

"I agree. You're a great dad and he'll be just fine." Brick opens his arms for a hug and I take him up on it. We've always been a hugging family and I have no plans on changing that with my boy.

"One thing that's gotta change is I need to move him out of the clubhouse. We're getting a lot more members and we're gonna need the rooms. Plus, I don't need him walking in on any of the Brothers with a club girl." That gets a laugh out of the both of us.

"When I was out riding the other day, I saw the new lumberyard just off the highway. They have those build-your-own cabin kits for sale. Maybe we should go out there tomorrow and see what options they have. The Brothers can help build it, so we'd just need the supplies delivered." And he's off. Sometimes I wonder if Brick's brain has an off switch. He can stare at any equation and solve it in his head. And books? Don't get me started. He can read anything and remember it forever.

"Not a bad idea. We can load up the little man and take the truck."

"I have the perfect spot for the cabin already in mind. It can go behind the clubhouse, toward the right side. We can pave a driveway around that side, so you can drive right up to it."

"I like the way you think," I slap him on the back one more time, "but get back to work. I'm gonna stay here 'til Connor wakes up."

"Later." And he's gone.

I try to sneak back into Connor's room, but I make it one step and his eyes open. "Hey, buddy, did you have a good nap?"

"Yup," he answers with a yawn.

"How about we spend the afternoon watching some cartoons?" That gets his little body wiggling so fast, he almost tumbles out of the bed.

"Reptar! Roar!" Connor runs across his room and grabs onto my legs.

"Oof! Be careful. Don't wanna break your dinosaur legs." I scoop him up and tickle him until he starts laughing uncontrollably. I toss him on the couch in my room, put the tape in the VCR, grab the remote, and sit down next to my boy.

I'm sure there'll be plenty of issues that come up, having to raise my son without a mother, but we can worry about those another day. Right here and now is all about me and him and *Rugrats* on the TV screen. I just want to enjoy him being a kid who actually likes to cuddle with his pops.

Before you know it, he'll be all grown up and leading this club himself. We'll figure out the rest later.

CHAPTER THREE

MOUNTAIN

EIGHT YEARS LATER

"When did they get so damn big?' Butch asks, taking a swig of his beer.

"Good fucking question," Skynyrd responds before I have a chance, but his answer is definitely not wrong.

I turn around to flip the burgers and brats I'm grilling. Today's a bright and sunny July day, and we're having a club family cookout. That means our backyard is full of Brothers, their Old Ladies, kids, club girls, and a few select hangarounds. I've got the meat on the grill and some of the Old Ladies and club girls worked together to wrangle up sides to share. It's not often the two bunches of women get along, but for occasions like this, I don't give them any other choice.

If a club girl was to say, or do, something inappropriate in front of an Old Lady or one of the kids, she would be up shit's creek without a paddle. I don't take kindly to bad seeds. They learned very quickly who takes priority around here, and it definitely isn't them.

Brrraaaaaappp!

Damnit, Connor! I let him out of my sight for ten minutes and he's already raising hell.

"Those boys are gonna give me gray hairs," I grumble to whoever is listening.

"That's why I shave my head. No hairs mean no grays," Butch laughs back.

"Why did we agree to let those boys get dirt bikes?"

"You got Connor his first, then we had to listen to our boys whine and complain until we gave in," Skynyrd barks back.

"Yea yea. They could be doing worse things. I'm just glad Connor is over his tree climbing phase. Two broken arms were enough for me." I think this kid was put on the planet to try and give me a heart attack.

I flip the burgers one last time and yell out, "Food's done. Come and eat." The group as a whole swarms toward the patio as I get the meat on the platters and carry them over to the row of tables.

Looking around, I don't see Connor.

Brrraaaaaappp!

Oh, but I can hear him just fine. Next thing I know, Connor and his dirt bike come whipping out of the tree line, and I wave my arms to get his attention. He must see me, because instantly the bike comes to a skidded stop, the back tire digging a huge rut in the grass.

I stomp over to him, and when I'm within arm's reach, I smack him upside the helmet. My palm hits the plastic with a thud and Connor rips it off his head.

"What'd you do that for, Pops?" He stares at me like I'm the idiot.

"You just ripped a huge chunk out of the yard with your little daredevil stop. If you would've slowed down the right way, you wouldn't be on clean-up duty after the party is over."

"Clean-up? But isn't that what the club girls and Prospects are for," Connor whines.

"And what exactly do you think you're gonna be in a few years? That's right, a Prospect. Just because you're my son doesn't mean you don't have to go through the process like everyone else who joins this club." I rip the helmet out of his hand and point him to the garage. "Go WALK the bike back to its spot, then come find me. We're gonna eat this food I cooked and hang out with our club, together. Do I make myself clear?"

"Yes, Pops." I hand him back the helmet and he starts his slow walk to the garage. You'd think I just asked him to walk to the moon. Dramatic much?

When everyone has a plate, and Connor reappears, I take my plate and beer to the picnic table in front of my cabin. I have the perfect view of the whole back and side yards. Every time I sit here, it reminds me of how lucky I am to have found this crazy group of people.

I've been home from the Navy for about a year now. Honestly, it's a good thing I came home when I did. Shortly after we buried my dad, things around the farm started to take a turn for the worse. We've been having a string of bad luck that doesn't seem to want to stop.

First, we had a bunch of cows die from some rare bacterial bug, then two of our tractors died within days of each other. My last string was when lightning struck a giant maple tree in the yard and it split clean in half. One whole half of the tree came crashing down onto Andrew's truck.

As a family, we decided to keep the farmhouse but sell the land. The farms on either side of our property split the acres down the middle. My mom, Sheila, was able to pay off the remainder of the mortgage and bills, with plenty of money remaining. Andrew and I lost our minds when she gave us each a hefty check. We both tried to give them back, but she wasn't having it.

A few days later, Andrew and I had a talk about what we were going to do next. I was twenty-seven years old and basically starting all over. Again.

"What about starting a motorcycle club like you always talk about? We have plenty of money to find a decent building, even if we have to do some fixing up," Andrew asked.

"It's always been just a thought. I never imagined we'd have this kind of money." The check had more zeros in a row than I've ever seen.

"That's how things start, Jethro. With a thought. Don't you have that chaplain friend you can call? He grew up in

a club, right?" I'm thinking Andrew may have put more thought into this plan than me.

"Malcolm grew up in California. He said he was around different clubs, but I don't know exactly what he knows or doesn't."

"Well then, give him a call and find out. I hope you saved his letter from last Christmas." I did. Malcolm wrote me a letter to let me know he was out of the service as well, and to hit him up someday soon. Looks like today is going to be that day.

So here we sit, over a dozen years later. The Rebel Vipers Motorcycle Club is flourishing.

My brother, Andrew, became my Brother, Brick. He's our club Secretary.

Malcolm King jumped at the chance to move here and help start a club from nothing. He now goes by the road name Bear.

My high school friends, Frank and Leonard, round out our original five members as Butch and Skynyrd.

One day while riding around, Brick saw a 'for sale' sign in the empty parking lot of an old meat processing factory. The next day, we looked at the property and were sold ten minutes into the tour with the real estate agent. We signed the deed to one hundred acres a week later, and we had finished renovations just over a year later. The five of us lived on-site while fixing up the main building, what we now call the clubhouse. We built bedrooms, bathrooms, and one giant kitchen. We set up a room for Church and filled the main room with plenty of couches and recliners. It may not look like much, but it's our home. We've updated a few things over the years, but that's all part of the club growing.

"What you doing over here all alone, Pops?" Connor drops down across from me and breaks my reminiscing.

"Just thinking about how the club started and that I'm glad you'll be in my place one day." I'm not sure how much a ten-year-old understands about what it took to get this club to where it is today.

"I know I've got a lot to learn, but one day, I'll know it all," Connor says with a serious face before taking a way too big bite of his burger and making us both laugh.

CHAPTER FOUR

LANA

Dear Lana,

I hope this letter finds you. If Mother doesn't get it first. You know how she is. That's why I had to leave the way I did. I hope you're doing okay.

I wanted to write and let you know some news. I just had a baby. Not what I planned for my life, but Mountain loves Connor so much.

Maybe you can come visit one day.

Miss you, Roxy

I refold the letter and gently slide it back into the envelope. I've been holding onto this wrinkly paper for ten years now. Roxy was right about one thing—our mother did hide it from me. She threw it away, and had I not accidently dropped a spoon into the trash, I never would've found it.

I saw my name written on the envelope and recognized my sister's handwriting. I shook off the coffee grounds and ran to my room to hide it. When I read the letter, I was nineteen and naïve, but it didn't take me long to figure out why she really left. When Roxy didn't blindly go along with what my parents wanted for her, they disowned her and she left. Our parents tried to do the same thing to me, and when I didn't give in, they tossed me out too.

That's what brought me to where I am now—sitting in my car, parked in front of a butcher shop, in downtown Tellison, Wisconsin. I'm so far away from home. Growing up in Florida was nothing like this town. For one thing, I'm nowhere near the ocean. The largest body of water I've seen on my drive was Lake Michigan. It's a beautiful sight, but until now, I've never been north of the Mason-Dixon line.

I tuck the envelope into my purse, climb out of the car, and stretch my sore muscles. Maybe driving straight through wasn't a great idea, but I wanted to find Roxy and get away from my parents as fast as possible.

"Can I help you find something?" I hear a voice ask. I turn around and see an older gentleman wearing a white apron stained pinkish red on the edges.

"I'm really hoping you can." I bump the car door shut with my hip and step up the curb. "This may sound like a weird request, but I'm looking for a man named Mountain. Would you know where I can find him?" There was no return address on the envelope, but the postmark tells what post office it came from.

"Did you say Mountain? You would be looking for the motorcycle clubhouse then."

"Motorcycle club?" What the hell did Roxy get herself into?

"I know it sounds scary, but the Rebel Vipers aren't all bad. They do great things and have brought lots of business to our town." This guy is getting defensive, and since he knows where I need to go, I can't push any more of his buttons.

"I'm sorry, no judgment here. I just need to find Mountain. Can you tell me where he is?"

"Sorry, ma'am. I just don't like strangers coming here and judging our people."

"I totally understand." This isn't the first impression I wanted to make.

Pointing to the right, he starts giving me directions. "Take a left at the stop light and drive a few miles. The road is pretty curvy, so watch where you're going. The clubhouse is on the left when you come around a sharp curve. It'll sneak up on you quick, so don't drive too fast, because you'll drive right past."

"Stop light, turn left, curves, and don't drive too fast. Got it." I hold out my hand and he returns my gesture with a handshake.

"Drive safe. If you get lost, just turn around and come back. Have a good day." One last wave and he goes back inside his shop. Glancing around the town, I get back in my car and head in the direction I guess I need to go.

That guy wasn't kidding about it being a curvy road. My car handles these twists and turns like I imagine a racecar would around a track. I hit the gas a bit early in the last corner and watch as two giant buildings become a blur to my left.

Luckily for me, there's an intersection just past the building that I can turn around at. I circle back and pull into the parking lot, which is fairly large and wide open. The only sign of life is a row of about a dozen motorcycles lined up at the edge of the porch in front of the building. I can hear noises coming from the repair garage located on the left side of the lot, but no one comes out.

Not knowing where to park, I pull over to the edge of the lot, get out, and walk across the empty lot. I'm stunned by how much bigger this building looks the closer I get to it. It looked large from the road, but it's even more imposing up close.

The double front doors are wider and taller than normal doors. I raise my hand to knock, but hesitate. What am I doing here? Oh, shut up. Grow some balls and knock.

Knock knock.

I wait a few minutes, but nothing happens. I go to knock again, but suddenly, one of the doors opens in and I'm face to face with a broad chest covered by a leather vest. Looking up, I see the most attractive man I've ever met in my life. My brain short circuits and I forget my own damn name.

Slowly lowering my gaze, I begin my visual exploration of this tall specimen of a man. This guy has to be well over six feet tall, and he's got shortly cropped, dirty blonde hair, and deep brown eyes the color of rich chocolate. His face is dropped in an annoyed expression, but I keep going on my hottie adventure. I can tell by a slight crook that his nose may have been broken a few times. A mustache and neatly trimmed beard cover what looks like a super sharp jawline.

His leather vest is over a black t-shirt and I catch sight of dog tags hanging around his neck. I wonder if I could convince him to dress up in his uniform for me. I'd show my appreciation for his service, for sure.

Lana! What the hell?

I quickly finish up my not-so-secret inspection and see he's wearing blue jeans and black boots. The outfit and attitude radiating off this man screams biker.

"Are you done undressing me with your eyes?" the man barks out.

"I guess so, but would you mind taking your shirt off so I can see what's hiding underneath?" As soon as the words are out, I slap my hand over my mouth and close my eyes. I can't believe I actually said that out loud.

The guy lets out what I'm guessing is supposed to be a chuckle, but it ends up sounding like a cough behind his fist. "Alright then. So other than removing my clothes, is there a reason you're here?"

"I'm so sorry about that. Apparently, my brain to mouth filter is broken." I shake my hands and cross my arms in front of my chest. "I'm looking for my sister. Last I heard from her, she said she lives here."

"And who's your sister?"

"Her name's Roxy."

The look that falls over his face is not a good one. His jaw clenchcs tight and his upper lip curls on the right. His eyebrows lower, forcing him to squint his eyes. I don't know if standing on this porch is the best place for me to be.

The door starts to close, but I throw a hand out, stopping it from slamming me in the face. "What the hell is wrong with you, you brute?" I shove the door open wider and it slams back against the inside wall.

The bang causes his face to change in an instant. He reaches forward and pulls the door closed behind both of us, joining me on the porch. "I'm sorry about that. Hearing that name causes a gut reaction."

"Oh" is all I can say. I have no idea what's going on right now.

"So, you're Roxy's younger sister?" he asks.

"Yea. I had a little situation with our parents and wanted to talk to her. They disowned me and kicked me out of my condo. I needed to get away, so here I am. She sent me a letter about ten years ago and this is where she said she was. Is she here?" Now that he started the conversation, I guess my brain's throwing it all out there to catch up.

He leans back against the porch railing and crosses one boot over the other. "Ummm, let me start by introducing myself. I'm Jethro, but everyone calls me Mountain. Roxy was my ex-girlfriend, and I'm the father of Connor, her now ten-year-old son."

"Was? What does that mean?"

"I hate to be the one to tell you this, but Roxy left us eight years ago."

"Where'd she go?" Shit. Now what do I do?

CHAPTER FIVE

MOUNTAIN

"Where'd she go?" The look on her face drops. She looks crushed.

I'm not sure how to handle a distraught woman. Since Roxy left, I've only been involved with women who know the score—one night at a time and nothing permanent.

"Why don't we go talk where we can sit and have some privacy." I lay my hand on her lower back and lead her off the porch, circling around the right side of the clubhouse.

Her body starts to relax a little, so I'm guessing that's a good sign. I point at the picnic table in front of my cabin. It's under the shade of a bunch of trees, so we'll be protected from the sun overhead. This is still my favorite place on the compound. The stress just goes away when I sit out here. We sit on the same side of the table facing the open yard.

"Since I'm the reason we're out here, I guess I should tell you who I am," she begins with a small laugh. "My name's Lana. Roxy is my older sister, and I haven't seen her in almost twelve years. Not sure how much you know of her past, but I haven't heard from her since she sent me that letter ten years ago."

I straddle the bench, turning to face her. "I know a little bit, but she'd always shut down when I asked too many questions. I just stopped asking."

"Sounds like her." Lana laughs again and gives me a peek of a smile. I can't say I don't like it. "Do you know where she went?"

I have no idea how to tell her the truth. The truth isn't a happy story. It won't end with a reunion and happiness.

"It may make me sound like an insensitive asshole, but I think I just need to rip off the Band-Aid and tell you the truth." She turns to straddle the bench and face me back. I just hope when I drop this bomb, she doesn't fly off the handle like Roxy did when she heard things she didn't like. "I didn't know it at the time, but she left me for her drug dealer boyfriend. She then killed them both when she crashed their car into a tree."

Lana is silent. If it weren't for the fact that she's blinking, I'd be worried she wasn't breathing. She's showing no emotion. There's no crying or yelling. She's nothing like her sister. She may have similar features, but if I didn't already know, I'd never think they were related.

She has the same blue eyes as Connor. That must be a strong family trait. Her eyes are so blue, they're like the sky on a winter day. Almost clear. Her hair is pulled back into a low ponytail and there are a few wild, loose strands around her face. The color is a deep brown, but the sunlight shows it also has streaks of a richer walnut color and brighter highlights mixed in.

To put it in words for a simple man like me, Lana is absolutely beautiful. I'm not sure why I'm feeling like this for her, but it's something I've never experienced before. I feel like a creepy asshole just sitting here, staring at her while she's lost in her funk. I need to snap out of this and make sure she's okay.

Her left hand is resting on the table, so I slide my right hand forward and place my palm on top of hers. The second our skin makes contact, she jolts as if struck by lightning, breaking the trance that she's under.

"Whoa. What was that?" Lana squeaks.

I shake my head. I have no words.

She pulls her hand back and I immediately miss the softness of her skin. "Would it be too much to ask if I can meet Connor? Then I'll leave and you'll never have to see me again."

"That's fine. He's at school right now, but will be home in a couple hours. Where are you staying?" She mentioned she was disowned, but I don't know what that means for her.

"I'll find a hotel nearby. After that, I'll figure something out." Lana stands and wipes her hands down the front of her jeans.

Do I be honest and give her directions to the nearest motel? Or do I use her unfamiliarity with the area and say there's nothing close? This could be my way to keep her close and get to know her better. We just finished a few more rooms on the main floor of the clubhouse. I could offer her to stay here, then convince her to be mine. She could be in my room and sharing my bed in no time.

"I hate to be the bearer of bad news, but there isn't anywhere to stay in this neck of the woods. You'd have to drive for awhile and I don't feel right letting you go off when we have empty rooms here." She starts to shake her head, trying to turn down my offer. "You can stay here for a few days and get to know Connor, then go from there."

"I don't know. I don't want to be an inconvenience."

"It wouldn't be a problem. I promise. Why don't I show you the rooms, then you can decide?"

I walk her inside and give her the choice of two rooms. She picks the first room on the left. When I find out she drove here all the way from Florida without stopping, I walk her back outside to grab a duffel bag of clean clothes, then she goes back in so she can shower before Connor gets home, and I head back to the picnic table. Images pop in my mind when I think of her showering in my clubhouse and they're damn sexy. Who knew soapy bubbles could be considered dirty?

About twenty minutes later, I hear the bus pull away. That means Connor, Adam, and Zach are home. It doesn't take long for them to come walking around the side of the clubhouse.

"Hey, Pops," Connor yells as he jokingly pushes Adam, and Adam pushes him right back.

"Connor, can I talk to you?"

He waves goodbye to the other boys and jogs over. "What's up?"

"Not sure how to say this, but someone's here to meet you."

"Who? Someone from another club?" Ever since we had our little chat a few months ago, he's been showing more interest in the business of the club.

"Sorry, son, no other clubs are here. It's actually your aunt, Lana, and she wants to meet you."

"Aunt? I didn't know you have a sister."

"I don't. She's your mom's younger sister. She seems pretty nice and has nowhere else to go." I see her walking toward us, and he notices my attention is elsewhere, so he turns around.

"Hi, Connor. My name is Lana. It's nice to meet you." She holds out a hand, but is left hanging when he just stands there, staring at her.

"Whatever," he mumbles and runs inside our cabin. The screen door sounds like a gunshot when it slaps shut.

She goes from cheerful and excited to somber and heartbroken in a split second.

"I'm so sorry, Lana. I can't believe he did that. I'll get him and make him apologize. I didn't raise him to be so rude."

"No, it's fine. Me showing up wasn't what he expected."

"That's no excuse. It probably has to do with the fact that he doesn't talk about Roxy." I still can't believe he was so awful to Lana.

"I understand. Maybe I should go anyways." She turns to head back toward the clubhouse.

I can't let her leave. I step forward and slide my hand down her arm, linking our fingers when our hands meet. "Don't go."

She turns around and looks up to meet my eyes. She looks so lost. "I don't want to go."

"Then stay," I beg her. I lower my head and she instantly closes her eyes. Her lashes flutter. My lips meet hers and she inhales a small breath. I step just a bit closer and feel her hand grip the front of my shirt. Our lips lock fully and my body surges with energy. One hand is still holding hers, but I lift the other to grab the length of her ponytail, tugging it just a little, forcing her head back even more. I suck her lower lip in between mine and slide my tongue inside her mouth. Her kiss back turns up a notch and she's with me at every turn.

I'm so engrossed in Lana that I don't hear Connor come back outside.

"Pops, what the fuck!" Lana tries to step back, but my grip on her is so strong that she bounces back against me.

I let go of her hair and tuck her as close to my chest as I can. Her softness and curves fit my callousness like a puzzle piece. I meet Connor's distraught eyes and am shocked to see tears. "Connor—" I try to say more, but he cuts me off.

"Leave me alone!" he yells and turns around, running straight for the woods. When he gets angry, he has a habit of going until his little body is out of energy.

"I need to go find him." I look down at Lana and she nods her head.

"I'll come help."

"Thanks." I need to find my son so we can figure this out.

CHAPTER SIX

LANA

"Pops, what the fuck!" Connor yells from behind me.

Why the hell am I rounding first base with my newly discovered dead sister's baby daddy? I try to disentangle myself from Mountain's arms, but his grip only gets tighter. He lets go of my hair, but tucks me closer to his body. He's so much taller than me, I practically slide underneath his arm like I was meant to fit there.

"Leave me alone!" Connor cries out and takes off running into the woods that surround the backyard. I'm not sure where he's going, but I hope he doesn't get lost.

"I need to go find him," Mountain whispers as he lets me go.

"I'll come help." It's the least I can do, since it's my fault he's running.

"Thanks," he replies and we walk toward the trees.

"Any idea where he went? I don't know my way around here like you do."

We reach the edge of the grass and Mountain grabs my hand again. "Follow this path here, but don't veer off it. It's pretty much a straight shot to the fence line about two miles in. I don't think he'll make it that far, but with his energy, you can't be too sure. I'll jog ahead and hopefully catch up with him. If I find him first, we'll circle back and meet you in the middle. That okay?"

"That's fine. If I find him, we'll stay put until you find us."

"Good, and after we find him, I'll paint his backside red. Then we'll talk more." Mountain leans down and drops a kiss on my cheek. "Okay?"

"Yea," I answer, not knowing what more to say.

Mountain takes off at a slow run, his long legs taking him out of my sight pretty quickly. I start my walk along the path, wondering what the heck I'm doing here. Not just in the woods, but in this town. Why did I think it was a good idea to try and find Roxy after not hearing from her for so long?

Roxy ran away with her drug dealer and has been dead for eight years. How did she get herself into that kind of mess? I guess years really can change a person, or I didn't know her like I thought. Mountain seems like a decent guy. Even though I've only known him a few hours, I'd like to think I wouldn't let some loser kiss me like that.

I'm getting worried about Connor. If we don't find him soon, Mountain will blame me. I stop and just listen to the sounds of nature. Wait, is that a sniffle? I turn to face the way I came from and hear it again. "Connor!" I yell out. No response. "If that's you, please say something. Your dad's looking for you."

"I'm up here," a small voice answers back.

"Where's here?" I look straight up, but all I see are the leaves of the tree canopy.

Laughter, that's a good sign. "Not all the way up. I'm not a bird, ya know."

"You can obviously see me, so help me out here." I put my hands on my hips and retort.

"Look left and up about twenty feet." When I do, I see two sneakers swinging back and forth over the edge of a wooden platform.

"How'd you get up there?'

"There's a ladder," Connor answers, leaning forward so I can see his face.

"While I got you cornered, I want to say something. I need you to know I'm not here to hurt or leave you. Now that I know you're here, I hope you'll let me be a part of your life. I didn't even know what Roxy did until I got here." He doesn't answer, so I keep talking. "Would you mind coming down so I don't have to look up so far? Your dad is tall, but this height difference is a bit much for little old me." Hopefully, he can get down without breaking anything.

"Fine. If my Pops finds me in another tree, he'll cut them all down. I'm not supposed to be up here without him." He disappears onto the platform again, then I see him drop down the far side of the tree. Quicker than I can blink, he's down on the ground and standing in front of me. "So, now what?"

"We stay here. Your dad will find us when he comes back this direction. Until then, I guess we sit and wait." I point at a row of bigger rocks at the edge of the trail, then I sit down and wait for him to decide what to do.

He stands there and looks at me for a minute before sitting next to me. "Why did you kiss my Pops?" Connor asks, scratching the rock he's on with a stick.

"I won't lie to you. I'm not really sure why I did it. But your dad and I are the adults, so we can do whatever we want."

That gets him to look at me. "That's dumb. I can't wait until I'm in charge of this club. Then I can do whatever I want."

"What do you mean?" Why would a kid be in charge?

"My Pops is the President of the Rebel Vipers MC, and one day, I will be too."

"So, because your dad is the President, that means you will be too? Like he'll just give it to you?"

"Of course not. I have to work very hard for the next eight years. When I turn eighteen, the club will vote if I can become a Prospect."

"What's a Prospect?" Never thought I'd be getting a lesson on motorcycle clubs from a ten-year-old.

That earns me an eye roll so hard, I expect his eyes to disappear into his head. "Sheesh. Don't you know anything about our club?"

"Nope. Didn't even know it was a thing until today."

"You have lots to learn if you're gonna be with my Pops."

"Be with your Pops? Who said I was gonna be with him?" This kid is jumping the gun big time. I can feel my cheeks flaming like they have a horrible sunburn.

"Why'd you come here to find my mother?" Connor does a major one-eighty in our conversation. Talk about verbal whiplash.

"You're a little young to know all the details yet, but one day, I'll fill you in. What I can tell you is that my parents aren't the nicest of people and they kicked me out of their lives." They technically are his maternal grandparents, so I don't want to say too much. He doesn't need to know that they disowned me because I refused to go along with my father's crazy plans for me to marry his forty-five-year-old business partner, all because he wanted me to get him access to the millionaire bachelor's money.

"So, you came here to find Roxy." Smart kid.

"I guess I wanted to see if she would even want to see me. After that, I really didn't have a solid plan."

"You know she's dead, right?" he spits out.

"I didn't before I got here, but your dad told me." I'm still a little in shock. It's been a long time since I heard from her, but I'm not sure how I feel knowing that she's dead.

"So, what will you do now?"

"Not sure yet. I'll talk to your dad when he finds us and figure something out."

"Adult stuff?" he asks, earning me another eye roll.

"You got it, little man." I ruffle his hair, finally getting a full laugh out of him. I think I might like sticking around here to get to know him better.

"Ugh! My Pops says that to me too."

"That's dumb," I laugh back with him.
"I agree."

CHAPTER SEVEN

MOUNTAIN

I jog for probably a half mile before slowing to a brisk walk. Connor couldn't possibly have made it this far without me finding him. Where the hell did my boy disappear to this time? I swear, if he climbed another tree . . . he'll probably break a leg this time, instead of his arm again.

Turning around, I decide to take an off-path way back to the yard. Maybe he thought he'd hide better in a denser area. I'm almost back to the path when I step over a fallen tree trunk and almost fall flat on my ass. Stupid decaying leaves are slippery fuckers. I'm just glad that Lana wasn't around to see me do that. It'd be pretty hard to impress her and convince her I'm a badass if I trip over a damn tree.

I make it back to the path, all limbs intact, and start my walk back to the clearing. I get a bit further before I'm stopped by the sound of full-out laughter. I try to hear who's talking, but I assume it's Connor and Lana, though any of my Brothers could be out here too. I walk slowly, trying not to draw any attention to myself, and finally see them sitting on a pile of rocks on the path's edge. They seem to be having a good conversation, based on the pleasant tones of voices coming from their way.

Quite honestly, it's nice to see Connor talking to someone he's related to. Everyone who lives in the clubhouse is considered family, but he's the only one who isn't being raised by his mother. The other Old Ladies and wives have helped me when I needed it, but it isn't the same as him having a mother of his own.

Brick and I have an amazing mother. She and my father were great parents. I wish my mom was still here in Wisconsin with us, but a couple years ago her health made moving away necessary. Our bitter cold winters became too much for her rheumatoid arthritis, so she and her sister, Sally, moved to Arizona. They visit us twice a year, but it's not the same. She would know what to do about this situation.

I'm not watching the ground at this point, so when I step on a stick and it cracks under my boot, they stop talking and look in my direction. I'm frozen in my tracks. With no word to either of us, Connor jumps up and takes off running again, this time back toward the clubhouse.

"Not again." I hurry forward to where Lana is standing. "Connor! Get back here right now!" I bellow out, hoping he can hear me.

"I know it's not really my place to say anything, but maybe let him go. You can talk to him when he calms down."

"What?" I'm stunned, half at her and half at myself. I can't believe she would tell me how to handle my son when she hasn't even been here for a whole day. Why don't I find myself mad that she told me what to do? What's this woman doing to me? I'm not known for being much of a pushover.

My size is only part of the reason I have the road name Mountain. The most obvious reason for the name is because my last name is Hill, and a mountain is bigger than a hill. But the real reason is because one day while renovating the clubhouse, Bear jumped off the unfinished stairs and slipped on a pile of sawdust, dislocating his shoulder when he landed. I laid into him about being safe and not doing dumb things. His only comeback was, *"If you yell any damn louder, you'll make the mountains around us crumble down."* That made me yell at him again about how we didn't live in the mountains, but at that point, it didn't matter. The rest of the guys heard what he said and it stuck.

"We talked a little while waiting for you, and I think he needs to be allowed to be mad. I mean, I show up and he catches us kissing before getting a chance to know me. I'd be pretty upset, if I was him." Lana has a point. Doesn't make his attitude okay, but it makes sense.

I wonder if she'll let me kiss her again now that we're alone. Hell, we did it once and she didn't stop me. Hopefully, I can do it again . . . and maybe a little more. I step in front of her and tuck a strand of auburn hair behind her tiny ear. She drops her head back and meets my eyes. Her sparkling blues are almost intoxicating—I could dive right in and get lost in their heavenly depths. Where in the world are these words coming from? I've never just looked at a girl and had these thoughts.

"Are you gonna kiss me again, or just stare at me like a creeper?" Her question breaks through any resistance I had, and I walk her back against the nearest tree. I reach down to lift her by the hips, and she jumps up, wrapping her legs around my waist.

"Hold your horses, Blue. I'll kiss you when I'm good and ready." Which has to be right damn now. I don't think a tornado could stop me from kissing this woman again.

I kiss her with no intention of stopping any time soon. My tongue strokes hers and I let my hands start to do some exploring. Her arms loop around my neck, so I have no fear of her falling. I brace one palm on the tree above her head and fill the other with the softness of her breast. It's more than a handful, and that's saying a lot because my hands are huge. I rock my hips forward into her center and it causes her to moan out into my lips. We fight for breath every few seconds and her sounds are starting to drive me insane.

Before I lose my mind completely, the brain between my ears reminds me I have a son to talk to, so I slow down before I fuck her through this damn tree. I move my kisses across her cheek and stop to let us breathe when my lips are just below her ear. I give her earlobe one nip and then back up just a bit. She drops her legs, but I keep hold of her hips until she has a proper footing on the uneven ground.

"I'd like to continue that later, but we should get back before someone comes looking for us and sees something they shouldn't."

"I agree. And you have a kiddo to talk to." Lana pulls her ponytail out and shakes her hair. She twists it around and wraps it into a messy pile on top of her head. Can someone get more attractive when they do their hair a different way?

Holding out my hand for hers, she grabs mine and we start our walk back. "Can I say something that makes me sound like a nutcase?"

"I don't think much would surprise me, so throw it at me."

"Would it be weird if I said I like your hair up in that bun thing better? Damn, woman, what you're doing to me."

"You like my hair up?" She reaches up and toys with a piece that isn't fully secured with the rest.

I stop us just before we step onto the back patio and spin her to face me. "I like your hair no matter how you wear it. I just happen to have inappropriate thoughts seeing it up like that. The access it gives me to more of your skin . . ." I trace a finger down her neck, from her ear to collarbone, causing her whole body to shiver as goosebumps pop up on her arms.

"Whoa, okay. I'll give it some consideration." She lifts up on her tiptoes and kisses me before heading inside.

It's time to face the music with Connor and try to explain why I want this woman to be in our lives after only a few hours. I'd wish myself luck, if it worked like that.

CHAPTER EIGHT

BLUE

"Damn it, woman. Why won't you just agree to be my Old Lady?" Mountain has been all up in my face today. He's trying to convince me that three days is enough time for me to be his woman.

"It's way too late. I'm tired and wanna go to bed. And mostly because it's only been a few days." Three days!

"Who fucking cares how long it's been?" His voice is getting louder every time he responds to my rebuttals.

"I do, you idiot! I agreed to stay here yesterday and you're already asking to make us official." I'm trying to keep my voice down because Connor is down the hall in his room.

"Damn right, I am! I need you to be mine. That's how things work around here. When we want something, we do whatever we need to get it!" This comes out in a roar.

I deflate just a bit. "What about Connor?"

That causes him to tilt his head to the side and squint his eyes. "What about him?"

"He hates me."

Mountain grabs one of my hands, lacing our fingers together. I learned very quickly that when he wants me to really listen to him, he holds my hand. I think it's sweet—a little cunning, but sweet. "He doesn't hate you. He's ten years old and doesn't know his ass from a hole in the ground."

"I don't want to start with him having a problem with us." I really don't. This relationship would implode fast if Mountain's torn in different directions.

"I talked to him this morning. I talked and he listened. He talked and said 'fuck' a few times, so I grounded him for the weekend. It's okay now, he knows how I'm feeling about you." So that's why Connor went straight to his room after dinner. He was quiet at the table and quickly asked to be excused. He's hiding from his Pops.

How do I get Mountain to understand that I don't know if I'm cut out for this life? I've met all the guys, and a few of the Old Ladies, but how the club runs on a daily basis is still a mystery. "I don't know anything about club life. I don't know what you do or how things work around here. This can't all be legal."

"You're right when you say you don't know everything, and I won't lie to you, there will be some things you'll never know about. The business we do is only to be known by the Brothers. It sounds chauvinistic, but that's the way things are done around here. I'm the President, and as my Old Lady, you'll be privy to whatever I tell you. But it doesn't go past you and me. You don't tell anything to anyone, not even the Brothers." He stops, taking a deep breath.

"That's a lot."

"It is, but you don't have to figure it out all at once. I didn't. The five of us original guys learned what we know one day at a time."

That makes me relax a little. If he wants me to be his lady, I would have years to learn as we go along.

"One last thing, and this is a big one. If I tell you to do something, I need you to not question me about it, you have to just listen and do it. I can't have my woman talking back to me in front of the Brothers. I need them to respect to me, and if you don't, that undermines my authority in this club."

"What if I don't like what you tell me to do?" I'm not going to rob a bank for this man, no matter how much I'm falling in love with him. Love? Where'd that come from?

He joins our hands and raises them to kiss my knuckles. "You wait until we're alone and behind a closed door, then you yell at me all you want. I'll listen to your issues, then try to nicely tell you why I did what I did. We'll figure it out together."

"Why does it sound so fair and unfair at the same time?" All this newness is coming at me so fast, my head might spin off my shoulders.

"Apparently, that's the life of an Old Lady in a motorcycle club. I didn't grow up in the lifestyle, but the people I know who did say that it's the ultimate test of a true relationship. Only the true and strong will thrive. And I think that could be us."

"But what about . . ."

"Just be his Old Lady already. Jeeze Louise, you old people suck at this stuff." Mountain and I both look to see Connor standing in the hall.

"Connor!" Mountain hollers at him.

"What?" he asks, crossing his arms. "It's true!"

"Get back in your room! I don't wanna see you until morning."

"Whatever," Connor replies, and the door slams shut.

"See! He even says you should agree." Mountain tugs on our still-linked hands.

I don't think I'm going to win this fight. Then again, being his Old Lady may just be the reason fate brought me here. Maybe coming here was all about me finding him. "Fine! I give in. I'll be your Old Lady." But I don't look at him as I say it, keeping my eyes on our hands.

"Blue, look at me, please." I've heard him call me that a few times but ignored it until now. "Do you know what it means for me to call you Blue?"

Looking up into his rich chocolate eyes, I reply, "It's my club name. Everyone will call me that instead of my real name."

"That's right. As far as the club's concerned, Blue is your real name. Calling you that is them showing respect to both of us."

"Wow." So much meaning for four letters.

"I need you to come outside with me." He pulls me to the door and I hesitantly follow along.

"Why do we need to go outside? I'm not dressed appropriately to be out here. What if someone comes out and sees me?" I'm only wearing one of Mountain's super extra-large t-shirts and a pair of his boxers. I have plenty of pajamas, but he insisted I wear his clothes if I'm sleeping in his bed.

"No one will come out here. I told everyone to use the front door if they need to come outside tonight." Well, that was thoughtful of him—depending on what he has up his sleeve.

Mountain walks us around the picnic table and pulls me down to sit next to him on the bench. "I don't know how to start, so I'm just gonna tell you why I wanted us here." He nods, I think more to himself than me. "This is where we sat when I realized you were someone I wanted to get to know. I touched your hand and our past connection faded away in an instant. I think that's what the jolt we felt was. Anything that happened in my past went away and your heart stole a piece of mine."

I don't know when I started to cry, but he uses his thumb to wipe a few tears away from my cheek. His right hand goes to the inside pocket of his cut and he pulls something out. I learned very quickly that his vest is actually called a cut, a mistake not to be made again.

"I like this spot," I laugh through my tears.

"It's been my favorite spot since I built this cabin."

"You still haven't said why we're out here so late. Couldn't this wait until morning?"

"Nope. This is where we first kissed. It has to happen here."

I'm so confused. "What does?"

"This." He uncurls his fingers and I see a surprisingly large solitaire diamond ring, set on a rose gold band, laying in the palm of his hand. "This was my mom's."

I stand up, taking a step back. "What's that?" I'm not sure I'm even awake right now. Maybe I fell asleep on the couch and this is all a dream.

"When I said I want you to be my Old Lady, I meant I want everything. I want you to be my wife." He pinches the ring between his index finger and thumb, holding it out in my direction. "Will you marry me, Blue? Please?"

I'm not sure what comes over me, but I just blurt out, "I love you!"

That sets him into loud, unrestrained laughter. Mountain stands up to join me. "I love you too, Blue. That's why I need you to be my wife, and sooner than later."

I find his eyes in the light shining from the porch and see that he's smiling so damn wide. My mind is spinning with so many thoughts, but they're all happy and have everything to do with this man standing in front of me. Why not marry him and be happy every day?

"Yes."

"Yes?" Now he's stunned.

"Yes, you giant behemoth of a mountain man. I'll marry you."

He slides the ring onto my left hand and I'm shocked how heavy it feels. I stare at it with amazement. "Thank you" is all he says before he attacks me.

CHAPTER NINE

MOUNTAIN

Saying thank you isn't going to be enough. I need to show my appreciation that she actually agreed to be my wife, so I basically pounce on her. She's looking down at the ring and I use her distraction to let my inner caveman out. I bend my knees just a bit, wrap my left arm around her ass, and pick her up, throwing her over my shoulder. The laugh that comes out of her is infectious. I laugh along with her and spin in a circle.

"Mountain! Stop! You're gonna make me sick," she yells, hitting my back with her fists.

Maybe I need to teach her what happens when she tries to tell me no. The plans I had to ravage her until we both couldn't breathe just went out the window. This may be a night for a slow seduction, if I can last that long. She'll be pleased in the end, but it'll be on my terms.

How in the hell was it harder to convince her to be my Old Lady than it was to marry me? I've had negotiations with some real shady people that were easier than convincing Blue to be my Old Lady. After trying every excuse she could think of why it wasn't right, I managed to convince her. She said 'yes'.

I swat her right butt cheek and she gasps in what I assume is surprise. "Calm your jets, Blue. We need to keep it down when we get inside. No use in waking up the boy and ruining all our nights." I head for the cabin's front door, and with one hand on the doorknob, I pause to make sure she's still with me. "Do you understand? No sounds until we're in our room."

"Yes, sir," she whispers.

Damn, I like the sound of that. "Good girl." I get us closed inside and head straight down the hall. After we're shut behind the door, I loosen my grip on her legs, letting her slide down my front, hoping she can feel what her body is doing to mine.

As soon as her feet hit the floor, I get the party started, grabbing the bottom hem of my t-shirt that Blue's wearing and lifting it over her head. Next, I slide my cut off and hang it on the hook just behind me. Then, my shirt is off and on the floor next to hers, and we're standing in front of each other topless. She's staring at my chest while I, on the other hand, am focused on her hands hanging by her sides. They're shaking.

"Can I?" she whispers, looking up at me.

"Nope. This is gonna happen my way. You okay with that?"

Blue nods her head and takes a step back. "Whatever you want."

"Take off your shoes and the boxers, then lay down in the middle of our bed." She's quick to respond and is on the bed in a flash. I use the time to kick off my boots and socks, unzip my jeans, and watch her naked skin glow under the soft light coming from the bedside lamp. It's the only light in the room, but it's plenty to see her perfectly.

"Mountain?" Her saying my name breaks me from the trance that her sexy body has put me under.

"Yes, love?"

"Is everything okay?" She sounds unsure.

"Everything's perfect. I'm just admiring the body I get to see every night for the rest of my life. I'm one lucky son of a bitch."

"Oh, okay."

"Be patient. I'm just getting started." I drop a knee to the mattress and start kissing up the outside of her leg. Her whole body squirms. "Stay still or I'll have to start all over," I say, still kissing higher and higher. She stays frozen, but I can tell it's not easy. Her hands are clutching the comforter like she's going to slide off the bed if she lets go.

When I reach her hip, I change my path of kisses and move closer to her center.

"Please" is another whisper. And just because she begged again, I move up her stomach instead of diving into her pussy like I planned. I'll get back to exploring that promised land after I kiss her until I feel like stopping. I lick and bite and kiss up the middle of her chest as slowly as I can handle, but my resolve is crumbling fast. I can't take it anymore, so I kneel back up, spread her knees with my hands, and wrap them around my hips. I drop down over her, propping myself on my elbows, next to her head. I'm lying one hundred percent on top of her, with just enough room between our chests for her to still breathe. I lower my head and devour her mouth. She kisses me back like it's our last day on Earth.

"Can . . . I . . . touch . . . please . . ." she stutters out when she can break away from my lips. She's been a good girl so far, so I think she can have one reward.

"Touch me, Blue." I barely get the words out before her arms are wrapped around my head and she's trying, with very little success, to pull my hair out.

I let her control our movements for a few minutes, but then my lips explore down the side of her smooth neck and shoulder. I keep going lower until I have a perky, rosebud-colored nipple in front of my face. I nudge it with the tip of my nose and it hardens even more. Moving up just a bit, I flick the tip with my tongue. Blue lets out a groan like she's experiencing the best kind of torture.

I've moved my left elbow down closer to her side and I'm using my right hand to explore. I reach behind my head and grab hold of her left hand that's scratching the back of my neck. I need to feel her hand intertwined with mine. Feeling her fingers in between mine calms my heart like nothing I've ever felt. I look up at Blue and turn her hand around so I can see the ring I slipped on her finger. Her smile is everything. I kiss her knuckles then let her hand go.

"I love you, Mountain," she declares as she runs her fingers through my hair again.

"Love you too, wife." I start my kisses again at her belly button.

"Not yet."

"Will be sooner than later."

"But—" she starts, trying to argue with me, but is very quickly distracted since my face is now in her lap. "Oh my."

I place one last kiss on her hip, then scoot myself lower, pushing my shoulders under her legs. Now that she's spread wide open in front of my face, I go to town. I lick the seam of her pussy and her whole body shivers again.

Using one finger, I separate her pussy lips and latch on to her clit that's poking out of the folds. I flick it with my tongue and Blue goes crazy. Her hands grab my head again and she pushes me down into her center. I keep attacking her folds and clit with all the vigor I can. Her juices are flowing, and I lap them up as fast as I can. Her taste is sweet and tart all at the same time. Like a glass of ice-cold lemonade on a hot as Hades summer day.

"Yes. Right there." I can tell she's having a hard time talking, because her words are mixed with hard breaths and panting, but I can tell it's a good thing because of the words she does get out.

Not wanting to miss the feel of her exploding, I slip a finger inside her swollen heat. I pump in and out a few times, then add another finger, stretching her open. Her pussy is hot, wet, and sucking on my fingers so hard, like she wants them deeper. I curl my fingers upward and she detonates like a damn grenade. It's the fucking sexiest thing I've ever witnessed. The pure ecstasy on her face is something I look forward to giving her over and over again tonight. Her body seizes once more as I pull my fingers from her channel. I bring my them to my lips and suck them one at a time, getting every drop of her taste that I can.

Now, it's time to let my poor dick out of his confines to join the fun. I scoot off the end of the bed, with the intention of just dropping my jeans and jumping back in, but my lady has other plans.

"Stop. Let me." Blue shimmies toward me and sits up on her knees. She grabs hold of the open flaps of my jeans, pulling me forward so my shins bump the mattress. When the denim is fully open, she pushes them down and I kick off one leg at a time. "Boxers. I like them." She's trying not to laugh at me.

"What?" I look down and understand why. I'm wearing black boxers with a certain red shirt-wearing, yellow teddy bear on them. "I can explain. Brick took Connor shopping for my birthday and they thought these were hilarious. I got dressed in the dark this morning to not wake you and must've grabbed these on accident."

Now, she really is laughing at me. Time to fix this. I put my hands on my hips and push those damn boxers down to the floor, kicking them toward the wall and standing up straight. The look on her face now isn't one of laughter, but I'd like to think astonishment. Her chin drops and she just stares at my dick like it's about to do a trick. The longer she stares, the more I feel the blood rushing straight down.

I take a step forward and she falls on her butt. She tries to get away from me, but I don't let her get very far. I grab one of her ankles and stop her from moving. She's laid out flat, so I crawl back on top of her. Personally, I like being naked on top of her even better. My hands and knees are holding my weight off her. "Open those legs for me right now, Blue. Don't make me have to tell you twice." She spreads her legs and bends them at the knees, opening her pretty pussy up for me again. I stroke my dick with one hand, and rub the tip up and down her slit, spreading her juices across my hardness.

"Shit, that feels good," Blue moans.

"Are you ready for me?" I continue to tease her.

"I need it," she whimpers.

Begging. I like it. I put a little pressure on my dick and find the opening of her pussy. I look up and see her eyes wide open, locked on where we're about to be joined. Her hands reach up for my shoulders and she pulls my upper body down to her, forcing my waist to follow the momentum and push my cock into her pussy. We let out a joint gasp and I lose my damn mind. The tightness of her surrounding me is almost too much. I take a deep breath to recenter myself, then slide further in. I rock my hips back and forth, each time hitting a little deeper, until I'm as far as her opening allows. I'm so deep inside her, her pussy is pulsing around me and I can feel it every time I slide back into her heat. She sighs and I decide it's time to kick it up a notch.

I grab hold of her thigh and hike her leg over my hip, allowing me to drop down inside her even more open legs.

I kick up the speed and use the fact that I'm on top of her to my advantage. Every time I thrust forward, I drop my hips and slam into her even harder. Her nails dig into my sides and I wouldn't be surprised to see evidence of it in the morning.

"Keep going," she barks at me.

Impatient little lady. So, I do what she says, and I keep going. In and out. In and out. She needs to know that I'm the one in charge here. Still holding her thigh, I move the other hand next to her head and grab ahold of as much of her hair that I can reach. I pull her head to the side and drop mine into her neck. I lick her skin and trail open-mouth kisses down to her collarbone. That's when I strike.

I bite down on her shoulder and she explodes. Her release comes out as a full volume scream this time, so I move my mouth to cover hers. I keep my thrusts going and her insides are massaging my cock like nothing I've ever known. I swivel my hips and it sets her off again. This time, it proves to be too much for me as well. The tingling races down my spine and I come so hard, my vision goes blurry. I pump once, twice, three times before holding myself inside of her pussy. I can't move, so I close my eyes and drop my forehead onto Blue's. We just stay still, breathing in each other's air.

"Well, that wasn't what I was expecting. But damn, I think I wanna do that again."

I open my eyes. "How can you be thinking right now? My brain is mush," I laugh. She giggles and I stop it by kissing her. I need her lips again. I thrust once more, getting a squeak in response, then slowly pull my dick out and roll over. I flop on my back and take my first full breath since this evening started in the kitchen, right before I grabbed the bull by the horns and asked her to be my Old Lady.

The bed shifts and I look down to see Blue rolling over, laying her left arm on my chest and crooking a leg over mine.

"You look comfy." I wrap my arm around her and tug her even closer, clicking us together like that puzzle piece again, then I grab her hand in mine.

"I am." She looks up at me and I lift my head, meeting her midway for a kiss. This one isn't sloppy or hurried. "Thank you, Mountain."

"What for?" I'm the one who should be thankful.

"For giving me a family. I can't wait to live this life with you and Connor." She's got tears in her eyes, but I know they're happy ones again.

"I'll give you anything you want. You're my Old Lady and I'll love you 'til I take my last breath." I kiss her once more and close my eyes, letting us drift off into the night.

CHAPTER TEN

BLUE

NINETEEN YEARS LATER

"BLUE!" I'm sitting on the back porch reading a book when Whiskey comes running out the back door of the clubhouse.

"Someone better be dead. I just started this book," I laugh at my own joke. The look on his face tells me something isn't very funny. "What's wrong?"

"It's Pops. He got in an accident. We gotta go to the hospital."

I drop my book and run for the parking lot. Just as we get to the front, Brick appears out of nowhere. "I'll drive," he says as we pile into his truck and fly out the lot.

"What happened?" I ask whoever wants to answer.

"Don't know for sure. George called saying that he just rolled in, and we needed to get down there fast." George is a doctor the club uses sometimes for medical emergencies.

I happen to look in the rearview mirror and am thankful for what I see—the road is filled with motorcycles. It looks like the whole club is following us. Two Brothers speed past and escort us the rest of the way. I've got a feeling that whatever happens next, I'm going to need all their support.

"The surgery went as well as we could've expected. He'll be waking up shortly. Just hit the call button and someone will be in." George—Dr. Green as he's called here—nods and leaves the room.

"Now what?" Whiskey's pacing at the foot of the bed.

I claimed the chair at Mountain's side, holding his left hand tight. It's the only part of his skin that isn't covered in bandages or scrapes. I can't keep my eyes off his face, waiting for him to give us a sign he's waking up.

"Whiskey, if you don't stop pacing, I'm gonna sit on you," Brick barks. The two of them are now toe to toe. Whiskey may be taller, and bulkier, but Brick is his uncle.

"Would you stop yelling?" The whisper makes us all turn to see Mountain's eyelids moving.

"Oh my goodness!" I jump to my feet and lean forward, gently kissing his forehead.

"What's going on?" The talking causes him to cough. "Water."

Brick grabs the pitcher off the rolling table and pours a cup. "Here." I grab it and help Mountain take a sip.

Whiskey runs for the door. "Nurse! We need a nurse!" he yells, to whoever will listen.

"Who needs a nurse? Why the hell am I in the hospital?" Panic has set in and Mountain is looking frightened. It's not an emotion he shows to anyone.

Whiskey is standing at the foot of the bed again. "Pops, you were in an accident. You dumped the bike and had to have surgery."

Mountain squeezes my hand so hard, I'm afraid I'll lose a few fingers. "What's wrong with my leg?" He's staring at the blanket covering him from the waist down. That's when I realize he's figured out what's going on. "Where the fuck is my left leg? Where is it?" He's hysterical.

"They had to remove it. There was just too much damage," I say as clear as I can, even with the sobs escaping. I've been strong, or maybe just numb, up until now, but my tears have started.

"Everybody OUT!" I think the whole hospital heard that.

Brick grabs Whiskey and they head for the door. "We'll find the doctor."

If fire could shoot out my eyes, my Old Man would have burns with his injuries. "I know you just woke up, and you're overwhelmed, but you're this Club's President. You need to be better than this."

He has the decency to look ashamed of his behavior, but I get worried by what he says next. "What if I shouldn't be President anymore?"

CHAPTER ELEVEN

MOUNTAIN

The gate rolls open and Whiskey pulls his truck into the compound. Damn, it's good to be home. Four months away was too long. The doctors and therapists didn't want me to leave the center until I was able to do everything on their checklist. I'm still getting used to this prosthetic leg, but I worked hard every day.

"You know there's a party waiting for you inside?" Whiskey chuckles.

"Yea, I figured, but it'll have to wait 'til after Church. We've got business to discuss." The truck stops and I get the door open, sliding out before he can rush around to help.

The doors are open and every Brother, Old Lady, family member, and club girl is scattered around the main room.

"WELCOME HOME!" roars out at me.

"CHURCH!" I bellow back, and the room laughs.

My Old Lady heads straight for me. She's pissed, but I try to intercept the fight. "Before you complain, yes, it has to be now."

"But we've been preparing all day," she whines.

"I need to take care of what we talked about the other day." I try to get her to catch my drift.

"Oh. Now?" And she gets it.

I nod, squeeze her hands, kiss her lips, and start my trek across the room.

As soon as the Church doors are shut and everyone's sitting, I start at the beginning.

"I went to pick up Blue's birthday present and stopped for gas on the way back. This guy was harassing a young lady standing out front, so I told him to fuck off. The girl managed to run away, but the guy got angry and was spouting off nonsense. I just left him there yelling.

"I didn't even get a mile before I saw a truck in my mirrors. It was approaching fast, so I slowed down thinking it wanted to pass. Next thing I knew, he swerved into me and I was going down. I could feel my left leg slide on the road, then I couldn't move. My vision was going fuzzy, but I saw him back up toward me. That's when I felt the pressure. He backed over the bike with me under it, then drove away. It happened fast and I blacked out."

"Most of you know already," Whiskey takes over, "but someone witnessed everything and called the police. Deputies arrested a man named Shane Miller for drunk driving and he's been charged with attempted homicide."

The room bursts in a mix of celebration and anger.

"Enough!" I slam the gavel and everyone quiets. "Next order of business. I've discussed this with the officers, but it's time to bring it to a club vote." I look at Whiskey sitting at the far end of the table.

"I motion for Mountain to pass his President patch to Whiskey!" Brick bellows.

"I second," Bear follows.

The look that crosses Whiskey's face is a mix of disbelief and pride. He instantly sits straighter in his chair, but then freezes. "Why now?'

"Because I can't ride. Therapist says maybe one day, but not any time soon. That means I can't be a proper leader. Now's your time to step up. You've been preparing for this your whole life."

"I won't lie and say I'm not hesitant, but I'll do you and this club proud." His eyes are locked on me. "Wait . . . what about Steel? He's the VP."

"There's just over a year left in his sentence. He called yesterday and I filled him in. He's good with whatever we decide. So, we vote. Everyone in favor, say 'aye'."

Bear stands up. "Aye."

Brick stands next. "Aye."

That's how it goes, all the way around the table. Every single Brother stands and announces his acceptance of my son becoming this club's next President.

That just leaves me. I stand and slide off my cut, holding out my hand. Butch hands me his pocketknife and I carefully cut the threads free from the leather. "Come here, son."

Whiskey makes his way to stand in front of me. I hold the President patch in my right hand and reach out to him, palm up. He places his hand in mine and we shake. I pull him into a hug and squeeze him with everything I have. I step back and look him dead in the eye. "Aye."

"That makes it official." Bear bangs the gavel. "From this day forward, until the end of his time, Whiskey is President of the Rebel Vipers MC."

"Hell yea!" This comes from Whiskey's best friend, and lifelong partner in crime, Hammer. He rushes Whiskey and almost sends both of them to the floor. Congratulations are made all around.

In this life, we don't get many 'happy' days, but this one is definitely up there for me. The day Connor was born is at the top. Second is the day Blue agreed to be my wife and Old Lady. Looking back, she said three days was too fast, but let me tell you, it was perfect for us. And lastly, today. Knowing my boy will be leading this group of crazy misfits, I couldn't be happier. I'll follow his lead until the day I die.

When things calm down a bit, I whistle to get everyone's attention. "I've one thing to say before we go celebrate." I pause, taking a minute to look around the room. "No matter what happens, we have each other. If anyone tries to mess with this MC, thinking it's going to be easy, they're poorly mistaken. They're going to have a battle. And before they get to us, they'll have one hell of a mountain to climb."

ACKNOWLEDGMENTS

N and J – Sometimes encouragement comes from the most unlikely places. Thank you both for pushing me to actually start this writing journey. My "naughty books" will forever be all your faults!

Rebecca Vazquez – Woman, you're an editing miracle worker. You make my gibberish sound like it belongs in the English language. Me and all my commas and apostrophes appreciate you so much!

Kay Marie – How did we get here? Getting to know you this past year has truly been an honor. Being able to call you one of my best friends is even more special. You'll always be "My Person". You are the Meredith to my Cristina!

My KM Alpha friends – Kay, Becca, Heidi, and Olivia. I owe y'all for so much. Thanks for being my "unofficial" sounding boards as I jump into this crazy thing called the book world. I know I can always count on you ladies, and I wouldn't trade our Alphaness for the world!

Charli Childs – Thank you for bringing Mountain to life. You are a design Goddess!

And last, but definitely not least, YOU! THANK YOU, READERS! Thank you for reading my first book baby. I hope y'all buckle up and get ready for more Rebel Vipers MC. The Brothers and their Old Ladies are excited to meet everyone, and I hope you're all ready for the ride!

ABOUT THE AUTHOR

Jessa Aarons was born and raised in the frozen tundra of Wisconsin. She has had her nose buried in books for as long as she can remember. Her love of romance began when she "borrowed" her mom's paperback Harlequin novels.

After experiencing a life-changing health issue, she had to leave the working world and dove back into books to help heal her soul. She would read anything that told a love story but still had grit and drama. Then she became a beta reader and personal assistant to another author.

Jessa is the boss of her husband and their castle. He really is her prince. Thanks to his encouragement, Jessa started putting pen to paper and creating new imaginary worlds. She spends her free time reading, crafting, and cheering on her hometown football team.

SOCIAL MEDIA LINKS

Facebook Author Page

FB Reader's Group

Instagram

Twitter

Amazon

Goodreads

Bookbub

Pinterest

Spotify

TikTok

OTHER WORKS

<u>Rebel Vipers MC</u>
Whiskey on the Rocks
Ring of Steel
Hammer's Swing

<u>Standalones</u>
Pure Luck – cowrite with Kay Marie

Printed in Great Britain
by Amazon